The Bipolar Journey:
Workbook Companion

A guided reflection and self-care workbook for navigating life with bipolar disorder.

by

Ivette Smith

TABLE OF CONTENTS

CHAPTER 1 – WHAT IS BIPOLAR DISORDER? 1

CHAPTER 2 – RECOGNIZING THE SIGNS.................... 3

CHAPTER 3 – NAMING YOUR TRIGGERS 6

CHAPTER 4 – MEDS, THERAPY, AND THE SYSTEM.............. 8

CHAPTER 5 – MAKING A CRISIS PLAN 10

CHAPTER 6 – SELF-CARE WHEN IT'S HARD 13

CHAPTER 7 – RELATIONSHIPS: EXPLAINING MYSELF 15

CHAPTER 8 – WORK, SCHOOL, AND GOALS 18

CHAPTER 9 – SHAME, STIGMA & IDENTITY.................. 20

CHAPTER 10 – CYCLES, SETBACKS & RESILIENCE............. 23

CHAPTER 11 – GROWTH & ACCEPTANCE 26

CHAPTER 12 – MY ONGOING PRACTICE 29

APPENDICES 32

A FEW WORDS AND CLICHES FROM THE AUTHOR........... 35

CHAPTER 1 – WHAT IS BIPOLAR DISORDER?

Understanding the diagnosis, its types, and what it means for you.

🧠 What I Know (or Think I Know)

What does bipolar disorder mean to you? How would you explain it in your own words?

____

____

____

____

📓 Which Type Describes Me?

Have you been diagnosed with Bipolar I, Bipolar II, Cyclothymia, or something else? What were you told by your provider?

____

____

____

____

❓ What Confuses Me

What have you heard or read about bipolar that feels unclear or untrue to you? What do you still want to understand?

____

____

____

____

____

📝 The Day I Was Diagnosed

If you're comfortable, describe what happened when you were first
diagnosed. What was that moment like for you?

____

____

____

____

💬 I Am Not My Diagnosis

What do you want people to know about you that has nothing to do
with bipolar disorder?

____

____

____

____

CHAPTER 2 – RECOGNIZING THE SIGNS

Understanding your unique experience with mood changes

✍ **Reflection: My Mood Journey**

Think back to a recent period of instability (either high or low). What did you feel? What were you doing? What changed?

____

____

____

____

____

⚠ **My Early Warning Signs**

These are signals that something is shifting — emotionally, physically, behaviorally, or socially.

Category	My Warning Signs
Emotional	e.g.
Physical	e.g.
Behavioral	e.g.
Social	e.g.
Category	My Warning Signs
Emotional	e.g.
Physical	e.g.
Behavioral	e.g.
Social	e.g.
Category	My Warning Signs
Emotional	e.g.
Physical	e.g.
Behavioral	e.g.
Social	e.g.

▣ Mood Tracker – Last 7 Days

Use this chart to observe patterns and note any spikes, drops, or triggers.

Day	Mood (1 = very low, 10 = very high)	Notes/Triggers
Monday		
Tuesday		
Wednesday		
Thursday		
Friday		
Saturday		
Sunday		

✿ Insight Journal

Have you noticed any repeating patterns? What helps? What hinders?

____

____

____

____

____

✓ What Helps Me Regain Balance

When I start to notice signs, I can support myself by:

☐ Reaching out to: ___________________________________

☐ Taking a break from:_______________________________

☐ Writing in my journal

☐ Calling my provider

☐ Practicing grounding techniques

☐ Other:

____

____

____

____

____

CHAPTER 3 – NAMING YOUR TRIGGERS

Identifying what sets off your mood shifts can help you prevent or better manage episodes.

🖊 Reflection: What Sets Me Off?

Think about a time when your mood changed suddenly. What was happening around you? Who were you with? What were you feeling?

____

____

____

____

____

🔑 Life Mapping: Stress Timeline

Use the space below to jot down or sketch major events, stressors, or transitions that impacted your mood. You could include job changes, relationships, health events, seasonal shifts, etc.

____

____

____

____

____

🔄 Trigger - Response - Recovery Worksheet

Think of a recent episode and fill in the chart below. This can help you identify patterns and prepare for future episodes.

Trigger (What happened?)	Response (How did I react?)	Recovery (What helped me come back?)

🍀 Insight Journal

What patterns are you starting to notice? Are certain people, environments, or events more triggering than others?

____

____

____

____

____

🔧 Coping Strategies for Common Triggers

List your most common triggers and one or two things you can do to cope with each.

Common Trigger	Coping Strategy

____

____

____

____

CHAPTER 4 – MEDS, THERAPY, AND THE SYSTEM

Make peace with treatment options and find what works for you.

🔖 My Experience with Medication

What medications have you tried? What worked? What didn't? How do you feel about being on meds now?

____

____

____

____

____

🛋 My Experience with Therapy

What types of therapy have you tried? (e.g., CBT, DBT, group, EMDR) What helped? What didn't?

____

____

____

____

🚧 Barriers to Treatment

What has made getting care difficult? (Access, money, time, insurance, providers, stigma)

____

____

____

____

____

📋 My Support Team

List the people who support your mental health and what role they play.

Name/Role – How they support me

____

____

____

____

👥 Speaking Up for Myself

How do you advocate for your needs during appointments? What would you like to get better at expressing?

____

____

____

____

CHAPTER 5 – MAKING A CRISIS PLAN

Preparing for the hard days so you (and your people) have a guide when you need it most.

📟 What a Crisis Looks Like for Me

What does a mental health crisis look like for *you specifically*? What are the warning signs that things are getting worse?

____

____

____

____

____

◹ My Red Flags

List the thoughts, feelings, or behaviors that signal you're nearing or in crisis.

____

____

____

____

____

📞 Who to Call and What to Say

Who can you trust to help you when you're not okay? What would you want them to *know or do*?

____

____

____

____

____

📋 My Safety Plan

What steps can you take when you feel unsafe or out of control?
What's helped you before?

____

____

____

____

🧍 What I Need (and Don't Need)

What kind of support actually helps when you're in crisis? What
makes it worse?

✅ I need:

____

____

____

✖ I don't need:

____

____

____

____

____

💡 Emergency Info Snapshot

Fill in the blanks so someone helping you can quickly access what matters.

- **Diagnosis:**

  ____

- **Medications:**

  ____

- **Allergies:**

  ____

- **Provider Contact Info:**

  ____

- **Emergency Contact(s):**

  ____

  ____

  ____

CHAPTER 6 – SELF-CARE WHEN IT'S HARD

Gentle tools and small wins for the days that feel impossible.

What Self-Care Looks Like to Me

What does authentic self-care mean to you? What helps you feel okay or grounded—not just 'productive'?

____

____

____

____

The Bare Minimum List

What small, doable things can you try to do even on your hardest days?

____

____

____

____

My Soothing Toolkit

List sounds, smells, textures, objects, or practices that help soothe your nervous system.

____

____

____

____

____

⬤ When I Don't Want to Take Care of Myself

What usually gets in the way of taking care of yourself? How can you respond to those blocks with compassion?

____

____

____

____

✉ A Note to Future Me

Write a message to your future self for the next time you're in a tough spot. Keep it kind.

____

____

____

____

CHAPTER 7 – RELATIONSHIPS: EXPLAINING MYSELF

Navigating connection, communication, and protecting your peace.

♡ How My Mental Health Affects My Relationships

In what ways has bipolar disorder impacted your relationships with family, friends, partners, or coworkers?

____

____

____

____

⊘ Setting Boundaries (Even When It's Hard)

What kinds of boundaries do you need in your life to feel safe, respected, and emotionally balanced?

____

____

____

____

💬 Explaining Bipolar to Others

What do you wish people understood about bipolar disorder? How do you usually talk about it—or avoid talking about it?

____

____

____

____

____

▢ Who Feels Safe? Who Doesn't?

Think about the people in your life. Who makes you feel accepted and safe? Who leaves you feeling drained or misunderstood?

✔ Feels safe:

____

____

____

____

✗ Feels unsafe:

____

____

____

____

📑 My Relationship Agreements

What do _you_ want from the relationships in your life? What are your personal "rules" for healthy connection?

____

____

CHAPTER 8 – WORK, SCHOOL, AND GOALS

Creating the community and resources to help you thrive.

🤝 My Support System

Who are the people you rely on for emotional, mental, and practical support? How do they help you?

____

____

____

____

____

📞 Contact List for Emergency Support

Who can you call when you need help or just need someone to talk to? List phone numbers and contact details.

1. Name: _________________________ Phone: _______________________

2. Name: _________________________ Phone: _______________________

3. Name: _________________________ Phone: _______________________

4. Name: _________________________ Phone: _______________________

👦⚕️ Therapists, Doctors, and Other Professionals

What mental health professionals do you see regularly? What kind of support do they provide?

1. Name/Role: ____

   How They Help: _____________________________________

2. Name/Role: ____

   How They Help: _____________________________________

3. Name/Role: _______________________________________

    How They Help: ___________________________________

💬 How to Ask for Help

What would be the easiest way for you to ask for help when you need it? (Think about specific phrases or strategies.)

____

____

____

____

____

💗 What Makes a Good Supporter?

What qualities or actions do you appreciate from people who help support you?

____

____

____

____

____

CHAPTER 9 – SHAME, STIGMA & IDENTITY

Tools and techniques to help you weather the storm.

☁ What Makes My Days Tough?

What are the common stressors or triggers that tend to make your days harder?

____

____

____

____

____

✄ Coping Tools I Can Use

What strategies, practices, or activities help you manage tough days or emotional storms?

____

____

____

____

⚚ Grounding Techniques

When you feel overwhelmed, what grounding techniques can help you stay in the present moment? (For example, breathing exercises, mindful walking, etc.)

____

🔄 When I Need to Reset

What can you do to reset or shift your energy when you're feeling stuck or overwhelmed?

🔊 How I Calm My Mind

What calming activities (e.g., music, art, journaling, nature walks) help quiet your racing thoughts or calm your mind?

💌 A Note to Myself for Tough Days

Write a message to yourself for when you're in a tough spot. What would you want to remind yourself?

22

CHAPTER 10 – CYCLES, SETBACKS & RESILIENCE

Finding purpose, hope, and drive when everything feels difficult.

🎋 What Motivates Me?

What keeps you going on the days when it feels like you can't? What things or people inspire you?

____

____

____

____

____

⌛ Breaking Goals Into Small Steps

When faced with big tasks, how can you break them down into manageable steps?

____

____

____

____

🎯 What's My "Why"?

Why is it important to keep moving forward in your journey? What's your deeper reason for pushing through the tough days?

____

💡 Finding Meaning in Small Wins

What small accomplishments can you celebrate even on the hard days?

📝 My Motivation Reminders

Create a list of quotes, affirmations, or reminders that can help you feel motivated when you're struggling.

 Visualizing My Future

Take a moment to visualize where you want to be in the next year or five years. What do you want to achieve, and what steps can you take today to move toward that future?

____

____

____

____

____

CHAPTER 11 – GROWTH & ACCEPTANCE

Accepting the ups and downs, and learning to be kind to yourself along the way.

The Ups and Downs of Bipolar

What have been some of the highs and lows in your journey with bipolar disorder? How have these experiences shaped you?

____

____

____

____

What I've Learned So Far

Looking back on your journey, what are some of the most valuable lessons you've learned?

____

____

____

____

What I Wish I Knew When I Was Diagnosed

If you could go back in time, what advice or words of wisdom would you give your past self?

____

____

____

____

____

🌱 Self-Compassion and Growth

What are some ways you can practice self-compassion while still working toward personal growth and stability?

____

____

____

____

🎉 Celebrating Progress, Not Perfection

How can you celebrate the progress you've made, no matter how small? What does success look like to you?

____

____

____

____

💝 A Note to Myself for the Future

Write a kind note to your future self. What words of encouragement would you offer to remind yourself of your strength and resilience?

____

CHAPTER 12 – MY ONGOING PRACTICE

Looking ahead with strength, purpose, and optimism.

What Does Hope Look Like to Me?

What does hope mean for you in the context of living with bipolar disorder? How do you find hope even on difficult days?

____

____

____

____

My Vision for the Future

Take a moment to think about where you see yourself in the future. What are your dreams, goals, or things you want to experience?

____

____

____

____

The Strength I've Gained

What strengths or qualities have you discovered about yourself as you've navigated your mental health journey?

____

____

____

____

____

🚀 My Next Step Forward

What is one small action or goal you can take today that will bring you closer to the future you envision?

____

____

____

____

💬 Hopeful Affirmations

Write some affirmations or positive thoughts that inspire hope and remind you of your strength.

____

____

____

____

✳️ Trusting the Process

How can you practice trusting the journey and believing that each step, even the hard ones, is part of your growth?

____

____

APPENDICES

A. Mental Health Resources

List of organizations, hotlines, and websites offering support, education, and resources for people living with bipolar disorder.

- **National Suicide Prevention Lifeline**: 1-800-273-TALK (1-800-273-8255)

- **Crisis Text Line**: Text HOME to 741741

- **Bipolar Support Alliance (BSA)**: www.bphope.com

- **National Alliance on Mental Illness (NAMI)**: www.nami.org

- **Depression and Bipolar Support Alliance (DBSA)**: www.dbsalliance.org

- **Mental Health America (MHA)**: www.mhanational.org

B. Medication and Treatment Options

Information on medications and therapies commonly used to manage bipolar disorder, along with a space to track your own treatments.

Medications for Bipolar Disorder

- **Mood Stabilizers**: Lithium, Lamotrigine (Lamictal), Valproate (Depakote)

- **Antipsychotics**: Olanzapine (Zyprexa), Risperidone (Risperdal)

- **Antidepressants**: Often used cautiously to prevent triggering mania

- **Therapies**: Cognitive Behavioral Therapy (CBT), Dialectical Behavior Therapy (DBT), Psychotherapy

C. Daily Mood Tracking

Keep track of your moods daily to recognize patterns, triggers, and progress. This simple tool can be used every day or as often as needed.

Date	Mood Rating (1-10)	Sleep Hours	Energy Level	Triggering Factors	Notes/Reflections
Example:	6	7	5	Stress at work	Felt anxious, but went for a walk afterward.
//____					

D. Journaling Prompts for Self-Reflection

Here are additional journaling prompts to encourage self-reflection and emotional insight:

1. What does balance look like for me today?

2. What's one thing I'm grateful for right now?

3. How can I embrace my emotions without letting them control me?

4. What's one small act of self-care I can do today?

5. What does my "best self" look like on good days? What helps me get there?

E. Additional Reading & Resources

Books and articles to deepen understanding and provide further insights on bipolar disorder, self-care, and emotional health.

- "An Unquiet Mind" by Kay Redfield Jamison

- "The Bipolar Disorder Survival Guide" by David J. Miklowitz

- "I Am Not Sick, I Don't Need Help!" by Xavier Amador

- "The Noonday Demon: An Atlas of Depression" by Andrew Solomon

F. Personal Emergency Plan

Here's a simple form to fill out in advance, providing helpful information for emergency responders or loved ones in case of a mental health crisis.

- **Your Full Name:**

  ____

- **Known Medical Conditions:**

  ____

- **Current Medications:**

  ____

- **Primary Doctor's Name and Phone Number:**

  ____

- **Emergency Contacts:**

  ____

A FEW WORDS AND CLICHES FROM THE AUTHOR

Phrases become cliché when they lose their original meaning or impact. This transformation typically occurs for a variety of reasons, each contributing to the gradual erosion of their power. But they still hold some meaning because, in many cases, they are actually a widespread reality.

One key factor is **repetition**. A phrase that resonates with people is repeated so frequently, often in similar contexts, that it becomes too familiar to carry any fresh weight. What was once insightful or thought-provoking now feels predictable, as the phrase loses its ability to surprise or inspire. It becomes part of the background noise, no longer standing out.

Another contributing factor is the **simplification of complex ideas**. We tend to reduce multifaceted concepts into catchy, digestible sayings—like "What doesn't kill you makes you stronger." While these expressions might feel comforting in the moment, they often fail to capture the complexity of a situation, glossing over the deeper emotions or experiences involved. Over time, these simplifications become so ingrained in conversation that they stop offering meaningful insight.

Cultural popularity also plays a significant role in the rise of clichés. Certain phrases become ingrained in the public consciousness, often due to their widespread use in media, literature, or by influential figures. Motivational quotes or phrases featured in books, movies, or social media can easily become recycled catchphrases, losing their potency as they are repeated endlessly across platforms. What was once a powerful message becomes a predictable soundbite devoid of the depth it may have once held.

Then, there's the issue of **lack of personalization**. When a phrase is too general or fails to resonate with an individual's unique experience, it can come across as inauthentic or superficial. For example, someone dealing with mental health challenges may find a generic "stay positive" message frustrating or alienating, as it doesn't acknowledge the complexity or the depth of their struggle. These blanket statements, though well-meaning, often feel hollow and disconnected from the reality of the person they are meant to help.

Lastly, **comfort and convenience** often drive the use of clichés. They are easy to say and offer quick, simple advice or consolation without requiring much thought. In moments of discomfort, people often lean on familiar expressions because they provide reassurance. However, while these phrases may offer immediate comfort, their overuse can cause them to lose their significance over time.

Now that I have excused my use of cliches, just for fun, I will give you some of them in a nice compact essay. See if you can spot them all.

Life with bipolar disorder can feel overwhelming, especially on the tough days. But it's important to remind yourself that you are stronger than you realize. Healing isn't a straight line, and taking things one step at a time is okay. Every step forward, no matter how small, is progress. Even when it feels impossible, know that you are making strides toward better understanding yourself and your mental health.

You don't have to have everything figured out today. The journey is long, and it's okay to rest when needed. Self-compassion is a crucial part of this process. You are worthy of love, kindness, and care, especially from yourself. It's easy to be hard on yourself when the road is tough but remember: you don't have to do this alone. There are people who support you, and reaching out is not a sign of weakness, but of strength.

The challenges you face do not define you. You are not your diagnosis. You are a whole, complex person with strengths, dreams, and a future full of possibilities. There will be days when you feel like you are not making enough progress, but even on those days, remember that growth is happening, even in small moments. You are capable of navigating this journey, and you have the power to create change, one small action at a time.

It's essential to be patient with yourself. Healing takes time, and that's okay. Some days, it's about surviving, and other days, it's about thriving. Take each day as it comes and trust that you are on the right path, even when things seem uncertain. It's okay not to have all the answers. What matters is that you're taking steps forward.

You've made it this far, and that is an incredible testament to your resilience. Each challenge you've faced has only made you stronger. Your story matters, and every step you take toward understanding yourself, even the smallest ones, is a victory. Give yourself grace in the challenging moments, knowing that growth doesn't always come in a straight line. It's okay to rest and recharge—it's part of moving forward.

Remember, you are not alone. You have what it takes to keep going, no matter how tough things get. You're shaping a future ahead of you, and you are capable of creating it. You've already demonstrated incredible strength just by showing up today. Celebrate your journey, and always remember that you are worth the effort. And there you have it.

Clichés are, in many ways, an inevitable part of language evolution. As ideas and expressions become more widespread, they eventually lose their impact when repeated too often. To prevent something meaningful from becoming a cliché, it's essential to express thoughts and ideas in fresh, authentic ways and tailored to the specific context. Doing so can preserve the depth and significance of our shared messages.

My hope for you is that you find the nugget of truth in each one and make it your own.

~Ivette

Also By

The Quick Guide to Self-Help: Practical strategies for Personal Growth

The Little Book of Self-Help: Sorting out the Big Questions

The Bipolar Journey

Practical Wellness Collection: The Quick Guide, the Little Book, The Bipolar Journey

Marriage: The Hitch and the Glitch of Wedded Bliss

On Being a Woman: Trials, Tribulations and Triumphs

Ageless Aging; Embrace Aging with Purpose

The Dark Web and Scams

Technology and Future Trends: Reflections on the Future of Technology and Society

Cracks in the Foundation: Dealing with Doubt in the Your Faith

Nature's Pharmacy: Growing and Using Medicinal Plants

https://ivettesmithbooks.com/